Eli the BIPOLAR Bear

www.theelijahfoundation.org

First Edition

Library of Congress Cataloging-in-Publication Data

Bracken, Sharon.
    Eli the Bipolar Bear/by Sharon Bracken; illustrated by Joshua Nash.
    — 1st ed.
      p. cm.
Summary: Eli the polar bear learns to deal with his bipolar disorder.
    ISBN 978-0-9746568-2-3

10 9 8 7 6 5 4 3 2 1

Printed in South Korea

The illustrations in this book were done in watercolor and pencil on
illustration board.
The text type was set in Adobe Jansen Pro.
The display type was set in Bovine Poster and Brody.
Designed by Joshua Nash

With Special Thanks to:

For Their Support

Eli the BIPOLAR Bear

Sharon Bracken

Illustrated by
Joshua Nash

Child Heroes Publishing · Norfolk, VA

This book is dedicated to Eli, my son, who inspired me to write this book for children coping with bipolar disorder.

Foreword

Remember the days when a mother would say about her son, "He's had too much sugar. He's bouncing off the walls!" and a father would say, "Leave him alone, he's just being a kid"?

Today, parents, family members, and teachers are improving their identification of behavioral cues that suggest something more may be going on with their children or students than too much sugar or simply an "off" day.

The days of hoping a child is "just in a phase" of sadness, irritability, or hyperactivity have long since passed. Indeed, if a child is described as persistently irritable, agitated, angry, sad, or even "bouncing off the walls," teachers and parents take notice and take action.

Bipolar Disorder in children, sometimes referred to as Childhood-Onset Bipolar Disorder (COBPD), is a mood disorder characterized by a disturbance of mood and energy, accompanied by a combination of rapid and severe cycling of manic or depressive symptoms. A child who has been diagnosed with Bipolar Disorder, therefore, may experience rapidly alternating episodes of highs and lows. Mania, a high mood coupled with high energy, may include symptoms such as distractibility, impulsivity, hyperactivity, agitation, and talkativeness. Alternatively, a low mood is generally characterized by extreme sadness and irritability. Decreased energy usually accompanies depression as well as a loss of interest in formerly pleasurable activities. Chronic irritability is characteristic of Bipolar Disorder in children, as the rapid cycling between highs and lows leaves little time for clear wellness phases.

Such behavior can be confusing to teachers and loved ones, who must cope with frustrating behavioral choices made by a rapidly cycling child.

Children who exhibit bipolar symptoms are often misunderstood, misdiagnosed, and mistreated. Fighting the Bipolar battle with her own child, the author of this book recognized the importance of appropriately identifying and properly treating Bipolar Disorder in children. This book represents the courageous effort to bring Bipolar Disorder, a disorder formerly associated only with adults, to the forefront of the childhood experience.

Eli the Bipolar Bear was written to facilitate the understanding of Bipolar Disorder in children. For the young audience, it is a story to help children understand their own confusing behavior or that of their friends or siblings. For the mature audience, *Eli the Bipolar Bear* serves as a tool to teach, explain, and illuminate a complex subject that is often difficult to discuss.

To be exceedingly clear, this book is not about labeling or stigmatizing children. This book is about assisting families, parents, and professionals in understanding and explaining to their children and students the behavioral components of a complicated disorder. The ultimate goal of this book is to help children better understand themselves, their behavior, and their choices. Author Sharon Bracken recognizes the importance of getting it right; that is, properly identifying problematic bipolar behavior in children so appropriate and meaningful action can be taken to treat and care for a young bipolar population.

In these rapidly changing, highly demanding, and increasingly stressful times, it is paramount we, as adults, do our best to identify, diagnose, and properly treat children who exhibit behavioral signs of Bipolar Disorder. The story of *Eli the Bipolar Bear* brings us one step closer to achieving that reality.

--- Susan K. McFarlin, PhD.

Susan K. McFarlin, Ph.D., began her education at University of California, Los Angeles in the interdisciplinary field of Communication Studies. She received her Master's in Counseling Psychology from University of Denver and worked in counseling and case management before she earned her doctorate in Industrial-Organizational Psychology from Old Dominion University. Among her other current pursuits, Dr. McFarlin works in the arena of operational psychology, consulting with federal agencies and private security companies. Dr. McFarlin lives in Washington, D.C.

Eli was a small polar bear cub who lived in a warm igloo with his older brother and younger sister bears, his Momma Bear, and his Poppa Bear. He was the middle polar bear in the family.

They lived in a neighborhood with lots of other polar bears. His aunt, uncle and cousins also lived nearby.

Life in his neighborhood was fun and exciting. Eli played with his friends and his family, and went to school like all the other polar bears, but Eli wasn't the same as the other bears....

When Eli was born, the doctors cared for him and sent him home with only the best wishes for his family. He was healthy and well in their eyes.

When Eli was cold, Momma Bear would make him warm. When Eli was hungry, Momma Bear would give him food. When Eli would cry, Momma Bear would comfort him. And Eli *did* cry! He would cry and cry and cry. Momma Bear did everything she could to make him happy, but Eli was not a happy bear. He was an angry, very unhappy little polar bear.

Poppa Bear also tried to help out when Eli was so sad. He would carry him around and try to make everything okay for his little polar bear cub.

As time went on, the other polar bears also would worry about their angry little friend because, as he grew older, he didn't grow happier.

The other polar bears noticed that sometimes Eli would be really wild and excited. Sometimes, he was so excited that he would laugh and giggle uncontrollably. Eli did not pay attention or listen very well when he was in this mood. It was hard to calm him down when he was so wild.

The other polar bears also noticed that sometimes Eli would be really sad or irritable and angry. When he was in a sad mood, he wanted to be all alone in his igloo and not play with his friends or cousins. And when he was really angry and irritable, he would throw things or start a fight. Eli had a temper! Sometimes the other polar bears' feelings would get hurt because he said mean things.

Eli was always happier, sadder and angrier than the others around him. His moods would change so quickly that it was sometimes frightening. So, the other polar bears were confused about Eli. His teachers, friends, and family could not understand why Eli was so happy and full of energy some of the time, and so grumpy and sad – or even really mean – the rest of the time.

So, Eli, Momma and Poppa Bear went to the igloo of The Wise Old Bear where Eli was asked questions about his behavior. The Wise Old Bear was concerned about Eli's deep anger and sadness and his really excited moods. After many visits, the Wise Old Bear explained to Eli that he was living with bipolar disorder. Eli and the other bears didn't know what bipolar disorder was. How did he get it? Could the other bears get sick from it too? Eli was scared!

The Wise Old Bear said that these challenges were not Eli's fault. He said that sometimes, when bear cubs are born, certain parts of the brain don't work well together. And, if the parts are not working together like they should, a little polar bear might have confusing changes in mood. Because of these moods that are really up or really down, a polar bear might have some problems at home, in school and with friends.

Polar bear cubs that have really up moods and really down moods, like Eli, are called bipolar bears. His friends and family cannot get sick because of it, but it can be unsafe and upsetting for others if Eli does not get help.

The Wise Old Bear told Eli and his parents that with regular help, Eli could be more like his friends. This helped Eli feel much better. All he wanted was to be like all the other polar bears. Eli didn't want to be different.

So, the Wise Old Bear gave Eli a bucket of special, tasty little fish he could eat every morning with breakfast. The Wise Old Bear said the tasty fish would help with Eli's big mood changes. He also asked Eli to come back and visit him once a week, so they could talk about how things were going. Eli was encouraged that he might soon feel better.

A few weeks later, Eli really did feel better. He felt more like everyone else. Eli laughed when everyone else laughed. He didn't get angry or throw things like he used to, and he didn't get wild and out-of-control as often. The tasty fish, and the talks with the Wise Old Bear were working! There were still some days when Eli felt sad and angry, but not like before. With time, Eli's life was much easier at home and his grades in school were better too.

Momma and Poppa Bear noticed that Eli made more friends than ever before. His friends liked and trusted Eli and wanted to be around him again. Even Eli liked himself better, too!

About the Author

Sharon Bracken is a native of Norfolk, Virginia. She graduated from Virginia Polytechnic Institute & State University with a B.S. in Family & Child Development. For over 20 years, she has worked in the various fields of child and family development, most recently in the arena of international adoption.

In Sharon's yearning to give a tangible gift to her son, Eli, who was diagnosed with bipolar disorder at the age of just nine, she wrote the story *Eli the Bipolar Bear*. Soon, other characters and stories were developed. Subsequently, Sharon founded The Elijah Foundation and Child Heroes Publishing as a means to help educate children across the nation and around the world.

Sharon has four children - Joshua, Elijah, Thomas and Kate. She enjoys spending her free time watching her children compete in various sporting activities. Sharon lives in Norfolk, Virginia.

Another Title by Sharon Bracken

Elle, the Little Lost Wombat is about international adoption. It is written from the perspective of an orphan and focuses on the adoption of an older child. It targets the child's emotions as she comes to terms with trusting and loving a new set of parents.

For more information about our organization

Visit our website at **www.theelijahfoundation.com**